PHANTOM
Son of the Gray Ghost

By C. W. ANDERSON

PHANTOM

Son of the Gray Ghost

by C. W. ANDERSON

THE MACMILLAN COMPANY, NEW YORK

COLLIER-MACMILLAN LTD., LONDON

The Macmillan Company
866 Third Avenue, New York, New York 10022
Collier-Macmillan Canada, Ltd., Toronto, Ontario

Library of Congress catalog card number: 69-18233

Printed in the United States of America

10   9   8   7   6   5   4

To Reaney and her horse, Gray Fox

CONTENTS

PHANTOM
Son of the Gray Ghost

1 • THE HORSE THAT HAD TOO LITTLE

"WHAT a rider that girl is!" exclaimed the gray-haired man to the younger one in the judge's stand at the edge of the outside course. "That horse was trying to stop all the way but she wouldn't let him. No whip and no spurs but she kept him at it and really lifted him over the last fence. Sheer will power I guess. On a good horse she'd be out all by herself."

"It's a shame she isn't better mounted," agreed the younger man. "I don't see how we can give her better than fourth or fifth and yet she almost made that horse look good."

"I still can't figure what she does," said the older judge. "Anyone else would be whipping and driving on a horse like that but there she sat as if she had the boldest jumper in the world. And she almost made you believe it. Most riders wouldn't have gotten him over the first fence."

The slim dark girl was stroking a bay horse as they stood beside a trailer. He wore a white ribbon in the browband of his bridle.

"You did well, Boy," she said, "real well. Of course it isn't a blue or red but fourth isn't too bad. You were scared all the way but still you did it. I asked you and you did it." Her hand went softly over the nose and muzzle. "If only you were bold and really liked jumping what we could do." Her voice trailed away.

"That's certainly right," said a voice behind her. She turned quickly to look into the kindly face of a gray-haired man who wore a ribbon in his lapel.

"Excuse me for eavesdropping," he said, "but I came around to see you and explain why we couldn't place you higher in the class. If your horse were as good as you it would have been the blue."

"I was happy to get fourth," said the girl. "It's not his fault that he's timid. He must have had some really bad falls at one time and it's taken all his confidence. I can feel his heart pounding through my knees. He's really afraid of the fences."

"Then how did you do it?" asked the judge. "He had a good round and you didn't use a whip or even your heels. Unless you watched closely you'd have thought he did it on his own."

"I talk to him," said the girl simply. "I tell him he can do it and then I ask him. He's afraid but he does it for me."

"He does indeed," said the judge. "But I think it's more than that. You've heard the old saying, 'Throw your heart over the fence and your horse will follow.' You certainly do that, but perhaps you throw it a little higher and a little farther than others do. I have to think so."

The girl flushed slightly at the compliment. "Sometimes I hate to put him through it," she said. "He's such a kind and honest horse if you don't ask too much of him. If only I could be satisfied with hacking and a small jump once in a while! But I love jumping—the speed and the excitement, with the fences standing big and solid. It's got me and I can't help it."

"It takes you that way," said the judge with a smile, "especially when you're young. It was that way with me, too. It never occurred to me that fences were for anything but jumping. I'd go looking for them, especially the big ones."

He paused and studied the bay horse carefully.

"For some riders this would be the perfect mount," he said. "Gentle, mannerly and dependable. Nothing to ever upset a timid rider. And so many riders are really timid but won't admit it, even to themselves. My granddaughter was like that and I didn't realize it, so I made a great mistake. I got her a horse that was too much for her—a lot too much. He made her so nervous that she is ready to give up riding entirely. What I should have gotten for her was a horse like this. Now, if it had been you—" He stopped and was thoughtful. Then he looked up.

"This horse I got for her is a big gray Thoroughbred. He's nervous and high-strung and a real handful. He was pushed too hard, too soon, and grew to hate the race track. At last they couldn't get him near it. I got him almost as a gift; they wanted to get rid of him. I felt that a bold rider with patience and understanding might make a fine horse of him—maybe even a great one. I still think so." He looked at the girl and noted how intently she had listened.

"Would you be willing to trade your horse for this gray? It would be a gamble. It might not work out but if it did you'd really have something. Would you care to make such a trade?"

The girl's eyes lighted up. "Oh, I would!" she cried. "That would be wonderful!" Then she hesitated, turned to the bay horse and put her hand to his muzzle.

"But I couldn't," she said. "He's done so much for me. I love him even if he can't go as far as I want to."

"I know how it is," said the judge. "But he couldn't have a better home or a better life. She'd love him as much as you do. And for him—no more shows and jumping. Just quiet hacking. Think it over. Give me a call and come over and see the gray." He handed her a card.

"It's a gamble, as I said. But you could end up with something special—something very special."

2 • THE HORSE THAT HAD TOO MUCH

ALL that night Sally dreamed of a gray horse—a big fiery gray that went like the wind and jumped unbelievable fences as if he had wings. The fences grew bigger and bigger and her spirits soared as flight and pace increased. When she awoke to the familiar surroundings of her bedroom disappointment came over her.

Then came the remembrance of yesterday; the kindly horse show judge and the offer of a big gray horse—a Thoroughbred. She leaped out of bed and dashed for the shower. This was no day to lie abed. This might be the day of days.

"There he is," said Mr. Jameson as a groom led out a big horse, iron gray except for black and white dapples. His head was up, his eyes flashed and his hoofs spurned the earth as if he wanted to be airborne.

A thrill ran down Sally's spine—she tingled to her fingertips. A flush of excitement was in her cheeks as she asked, "Can I try him?"

Mr. Jameson looked at her intently. "Good girl," he said. "I thought you'd feel that way. You're not nervous?"

"He's wonderful," she said breathlessly. "I love him."

"Saddle him, Joe," said Mr. Jameson.

"Snaffle or double bridle?" asked the groom.

Mr. Jameson turned to Sally. "You really can't hold him in the way he is now," he said, "not with the toughest curb. I'd use a snaffle; it's more like the racing bit he's used to. With your light hands you might ease him a bit without making him fight you."

"I'll try," said Sally. "I may have to go faster than I should. I'll have to go along with him and not upset him but I'll try to bring him back not too hot."

"And that's all you're thinking of?" said Mr. Jameson. "Just the horse?" He put a gentle hand on her shoulder. "You warm an old horseman's heart. I didn't know there were any more like you left."

It was a long time before Mr. Jameson and the groom saw a horse and rider top the ridge of the hill beyond the meadow. Even at that distance they could see that there was an accord between the two. As they came nearer it was apparent that the gray horse, still full of himself, was not fighting his rider.

"She sits him like she was born there," said the groom. "Not pulling an ounce but she's got that big boy right in her lap."

"She's a natural, Joe. Like you were when you were younger," he said. And then with a smile at the groom, "And maybe even a little better."

"Quite a bit better," said the groom. "I learned but

"There he is," said Mr. Jameson. His head was up, his eyes flashed and his hoofs seemed to spurn the earth as if he wanted to be airborne.

this one, she was born with it. You can see that. They talk to her and she understands."

"Sit down," said Mr. Jameson when they came to a seat built around a big oak. "I feel you should know all about this horse, at least as much as I can tell you, before you make up your mind. There are a lot of 'ifs.' On breeding you can't fault him. He's by Native Dancer and out of a fine mare. That sort of breeding would be priceless if there wasn't a 'hole in him,' as horsemen say. And it's there. I want you to realize that."

He paused for a moment to collect his thoughts. "Maybe the trouble was the way he was handled. I think it was. If that's so then with patience he can be straightened out. If it's an erratic streak in him it might get worse. That's the gamble."

Sally nodded. "I understand," she said. "But he didn't seem like that. Just nervous and all wound up."

"That's what I think. He was pushed too hard, too soon, and he grew to hate the race track and the training. The man who had him was a hard taskmaster; a horse had to be tough to take it. And this one wouldn't take it. One look at his eye will tell you that."

"Yes," said Sally. "I could feel that."

"I have a notion that with an entirely different life

he can be a different horse. But it will take special handling. Someone who is firm but gentle and understanding. And without fear. That's absolutely essential. A nervous rider would never get along with this horse."

"And you think I could do it?" asked Sally.

"Better than anyone I know," he answered.

"Then I'd like to try," said Sally.

Mr. Jameson stood up and shook hands. "Good luck, then. You may need it." Then he paused. "But maybe not," he added. "I think you're the sort that make their own luck."

3 • HIS OWN WAY

THE big gray crossed the wide meadow in a sweeping gallop as Sally sat close to the saddle, leaning forward to the power of that surging drive. Her hair streamed behind as her hands kept a light, steady pressure on the reins. She was not sure if she had any control but since he was not wide open she hoped it was in response to the reins. A badger hole showed ahead and when the horse swung aside in response to pressure of knee and rein Sally felt her spirits rise. So she wasn't just a passenger; headlong though the pace was. Possibly this was just his idea of a canter.

Sally's eyes glowed with excitement. He had to do things this way. It was the way he was made. He was like a car that had only one speed—no low or intermediate, only high. And you couldn't change him; you had to go along. At least at first—and maybe always.

A field away Sally saw a horseman. The gray saw him too, for he snorted through flaring nostrils. As they came closer Sally recognized Mr. Jameson.

"I thought that was you when I first caught sight of you," he said. "Nobody but Phantom goes like that."

"I know I was going too fast," said Sally. "But that seems to be the way he wants it. I tried to take a hold but he began to fight the bit so I thought I'd better go along his way for now."

"I think it's the only way," said Mr. Jameson. "Give him a chance to get to know you and trust you and he may give in a little. He may not always be a rebel if there's nothing to fight about."

Mr. Jameson studied the gray horse intently. "He looks right," he said at last. "Not content—he's not that sort of a horse, but not upset. I think he already knows that you two are alike; that you both want to do things in a big way and that nothing he does frightens you or makes you nervous—that when he's so full of himself he has to let go and get rid of some of it, you'll understand and go with him. That may take you on some pretty fast rides but no harm will come of it if you keep cool."

"Oh, I won't mind," said Sally. "I love all that speed and power. He can go as fast as he wants if it won't hurt him."

"It won't hurt him. He's no wild-eyed crazy sort. It's just that he's geared for another world. Look at that shoulder and those quarters. They were not made for walking or jogging. They were made to run everything into the ground that tried to go along with him, only something went wrong along the way. He got to hate the world he was born into and now you've got to find another life for him."

"That sounds like quite a job," said Sally soberly. "How shall I begin?"

"Go along with him just as you are. As he gets to

"I thought he would go right through the fence, when he let go with the most terrific jump I ever saw!"

know you and trust you, try to get him to give in a little. It won't be much at first; he may never give you just what you ask for—it will probably always be more. But if you can keep him down a little you might go far with him."

"I'm trying," said Sally, "and sometimes it seems he is giving in just a little."

"I saw that when you came up. He was carrying a steady head; not trying to get away from the bit. You're on the right track. But there's one thing—" He paused.

"Am I doing something wrong?" asked Sally anxiously.

"Not at all. I just want to warn you about something. Don't try to jump him—not for a long time. It might be dangerous."

"Oh, I won't," said Sally. "Not until you tell me I can."

"When he first came I put him in our big paddock," said Mr. Jameson. "He was all steamed up when he came off the van and I thought a gallop around the paddock would relax him. He went around twice, wide open, and then headed for the other end. I thought he would go right through the fence, when he let go with the most terrific jump I ever saw! That fence was a full five feet and he cleared it with a foot to spare. And at that speed—not even a steeplechaser jumps at that speed. If he had ever hit that fence—"

"Oh, he might have been killed!" exclaimed Sally, pale at the thought. "I'll never let him try that."

Mr. Jameson looked at her strangely. "Yes, he might have been killed. So you see why you mustn't try a jump. Not until he knows the difference between a hand gallop and a dead run—and will give you what you ask for."

4 • NATIVE DANCER

SALLY led Phantom to the mounting block. She was her own groom; everything about the stable was her own responsibility and she liked it that way. She noticed how often the hours spent around the stable when she was alone with a horse brought a closer relationship than even riding did. She also realized that the horse really belonged to the one who cared for him; fed him when he was hungry, watered him when he was thirsty and rubbed him down when he was warm and sweaty.

With a horse like Phantom it was doubly important to be with him as much as possible. She had groomed him slowly and carefully, talking quietly to him all the time. When she found he flinched at the body brush she changed to a soft rag. He had a thin skin that quivered at her touch but her gentle hands and soft voice eventually calmed him. When she noticed again how he was aquiver at the mere sight of the saddle she knew there was much that had to be rubbed from his mind. He must have had some very bad times under the saddle and he was still not sure that things would be different now.

His sixteen-and-a-half hands made the stirrup much too high for Sally to mount from the ground and she had soon realized that he had always been held when being mounted and had never been taught to stand quietly and wait for his rider. Each day mounting had been more difficult and she realized something must be done or she would soon be left afoot. She remembered the advice of a horseman that a horse with this habit can only be cured by repeatedly taking him back to the mounting block until at last he is so bored by the repetition that he will do what is asked. So each

time Phantom moved away as her foot reached for the
stirrup she brought him back.

After a half hour the gray horse eventually realized
that this would go on forever unless he was obedient
and he let Sally get into the saddle before he started
off. Several times more she brought him back and
finally he stood until she was firmly settled in the
saddle. Then Sally leaned forward and gave him a
piece of sugar and patted him. Three times more she
brought him back and rewarded him when he stood
waiting until she was set. Then she knew that this
problem was solved, for a horse never forgets.

Phantom wanted to go into a gallop at once and it
was with difficulty she kept him to a twisting, bouncing
jog until they reached the open fields. Then he was
off and she had to content herself with the thought that
he was not wide open. It was but scant comfort, however, for the margin was very small. Even after several
miles the pace moderated very little. The great reaching stride seemed tireless. When they got back to the
stable he was still fresh and full of himself.

Rubbing him down she found he was almost dry
except under the saddle. All that galloping seemed to
have taken nothing out of him.

"Oh, you Phantom," said Sally stroking the shining neck, "will you ever learn enough is enough?"

At lunch she asked her father about Native Dancer. She remembered he had spoken of the horse although his interest was golf, not horses.

"I only saw him on television," he said, "but something about him made me always watch for his races. He was gray, so you could always spot him, and I liked the way he ran; he seemed to stretch out so. Even when he was way back you felt he was going to win. He seemed to have something special—like a champion golfer—you have only to see his swing and you know he's the one."

Sally was thrilled. "He's the sire of my new horse," she said. "I want to find out all about him. I'll go and look in the library."

"It shouldn't be hard," said her father. "They say he was one of the greatest."

Seated at a table in the library she opened the book she had selected from the shelf. Turning the pages she soon found what she was looking for.

"Native Dancer was a gray horse by Polynesian,"

she read, "out of Geisha who was by the great Discovery. Polynesian was best suited to the middle distances. He won the Preakness but the added furlong of the Derby was too much for him. His son, Native Dancer, was a true stayer, however, and two miles was the same as six furlongs to him. This added stamina undoubtedly came from his dam who carried the Fair Play blood—always potent for stamina as well as speed.

"Native Dancer was unbeaten at two and completely dominated that division. At three he was equally brilliant and with a little better racing luck he would have been undefeated. In the Derby he failed to catch the winner, Dark Star, by inches, after being blocked at the head of the stretch.

"Horsemen say his stride was only second to that of Man o' War, whose twenty-eight-foot stride was the longest ever seen on the track.

"His length of stride made him seem to glide over the ground, hence his nickname, 'The Gray Ghost.' He was beyond a doubt one of the truly great horses of recent years."

Sally's eyes were shining when she closed the book. So that was the blood she had in Phantom! When she started for home she walked on air.

5 • PEACE AND QUIET

In addition to the fields and meadows that stretched on and on there was a large wooded area near Sally's home with miles of bridle paths winding through. Sally had always loved these woods; there was such a soft peace under the great trees, with only the song of birds to break the stillness.

Since the trail wound through the trees, with many sharp turns, she found that Phantom had to reduce his impetuous pace of his own accord. Soon she realized that he was looking around and noticing everything with great interest: the squirrels and birds and occasional rabbits that scurried off into the underbrush.

Through the reins she felt him relax—he still went as fast as the going permitted, but there was no tension. Apparently here was peace and quiet such as he had never known. Always before Sally had felt that his eyes were fixed on some spot on the far horizon and he was intent on getting there as soon as possible. Now, with soft turf beneath his feet and cool shadows from the big trees he seemed a different horse.

Maybe this was the answer, or at least a part of the answer, something as different from the things he had grown to hate as possible. Mile after mile they went, the big horse's gait smooth, powerful, and so rhythmic that Sally sat close to the saddle effortlessly and rocked along with the movement. This was complete happiness for her as through the reins she felt a response she had not gotten before. On the lightest pressure he

Through the reins she felt him relax—apparently here was peace and quiet such as he had never known.

swung aside to avoid a rock or a projecting tree root.

Now they were a team; she no longer was just a passenger. Phantom was beginning to respond and give just what she asked for. Not in the open fields— that was still far away, but now she felt this too would come in time. She mustn't ask too much too soon. Feeling all that power under her she knew it would have to be his decision and his alone. All she could do was go along; ask only when she knew he would not refuse, and hope. But as she felt the gray horse's response to the peace and quiet of the woods, that she loved so much, her spirits soared. They were alike in this! Maybe they could learn to see things the same way in other things. She would try to see things his way—through his eyes, and when he got to know her well enough he might be willing to do things her way. At least a little. Maybe enough.

When at last she saw the open fields at the end of the road she involuntarily set herself for the headlong pace that such going always brought on. This time it wasn't quite the same. She felt that Phantom regretted leaving the woods just as she did. He started off at an open gallop but kept veering right. Puzzled she let him have his head. At this point he always headed for home and at his best pace. Soon she realized he was heading back for the woods. He wanted to go back the same way!

As soon as they were under the big trees he slowed down a little so he could make the turns in the path. Sally leaned forward and patted his neck.

"Oh, Phantom!" she cried happily. "You love this just as much as I do, don't you? Maybe we *are* just alike. When you've had your fill of speed and excitement you want this. Just peace and quiet and everything soft and cool and green."

A bird call was heard and then a trill of silvery notes in answer. Phantom's hoofbeats on the soft moss were like a muffled drum and Sally's heart carried its own counter rhythm.

6 · STORM AND WATER JUMP

A FEW days later Sally and Phantom again took the
wood road. When they came out from under the trees
into the brilliant sunlight she was blinded for a moment. Her spirits were high for again Phantom had
gone perfectly; fast of course, but with a feeling of
relaxation instead of tension. As Sally's eyes grew ac-
customed to the brightness she saw a mounted figure

ahead but it was not until she heard the voice that she recognized Mr. Jameson.

"Hello," he called. "I wouldn't have thought that your wild fellow would slow down enough to make the turns in there. You're really doing well."

"I wasn't sure at first, but he loves it," said Sally. "He's a different horse in the woods. You can feel him relax as soon as he's in the shade of the trees. And you know he looks around and notices things just as a person would." She smiled. "Do you know what my little sister said when I told her? She said, 'He's a woodsy horse.' She meant he loves nature."

Mr. Jameson laughed. "She may have something there," he said. "If he was fed up with the race track— all that bustle and hurry and drive—where would you find anything so completely different? That's where I always ride if I'm all wound up or something is bothering me. When I come out the other end everything seems different. Maybe it does the same for him. From his looks I would say it does."

He turned toward Sally and looked at her keenly. "But the fences," he said, "are they still standing big and solid, calling for a real pace and a big thrust?"

Sally laughed. "I haven't changed and I guess I never will. I still see them in my dreams but now it's different. Before I had a horse that didn't have enough and I knew deep down that he never would have enough. But now I've got one that has too much—a lot too much. I know you can't add anything when they haven't got enough. But when you have too much anything can happen. It isn't hard to wait when you know you have too much."

"You've come a long way," said Mr. Jameson. "You already know what many people never learn. Patience and understanding come slowly to most people—sometimes never. Just keep on as you are going and I know I'll see a lot of you two. You'll make me proud of you."

The sun was bright that afternoon but there was a strange feeling in the air. Only a low bank of clouds showed on the far horizon but Phantom seemed uneasy and snorted softly as he tossed his head. Even in the woods he did not relax and Sally could feel the tension. Every little thing startled him: a bird flying or a squirrel leaping from branch to branch, which surprised Sally for despite his fire and eagerness he was not a spooky horse.

Before they were halfway through the woods the sun was suddenly gone and everything seemed dark and mysterious. There was no relaxed pace for the big gray horse now; he went faster than Sally liked on that winding bridle path. When she caught a glimpse of the sky through the trees it was dark and ominous.

Then a sudden flash lighted up the dark woods and a loud clap of thunder brought a wild leap from Phantom and a full gallop. Fortunately they were almost out of the woods and the path before them was fairly straight.

As they tore out from under the trees and onto the open meadow Sally was trying her utmost to restrain the big gray. She realized he was not wide open—he was not running away—but the margin was much too close for comfort, for he was frightened. She tried to head him on their usual path that led to a small bridge over a wide brook but he would have none of it. He was taking the shortest way to the safety of his stable. The fact that a brook lay in his path meant nothing to him now.

Sally, sitting crouched over his withers, saw that they were coming to the brook at its widest part, and at a wild pace. She had never jumped water; never jumped anything at such a pace. Her heart skipped a beat and raced on.

A length from the bank she felt the tremendous thrust as he took off. The brook was far below them and she scarcely felt him land as he galloped on.

"What a horse you are, Phantom!" she cried aloud. "You're wonderful—just wonderful!"

The stable loomed ahead and the gray slid to a stop before the door. Sally slipped off and hurried inside with Phantom as the deluge broke. Then came the rattle of hail on the roof.

The big gray was aquiver at the noise the hail made on the low roof and it was not until he was rubbed down and had received an extra quota of carrots and sugar that he relaxed.

When Sally walked to the house at last she was talking softly to herself. "Thirty feet it must have been," she said in an awed voice, "and maybe more. And high —high enough to clear the biggest fence ever."

A length from the bank she felt the tremendous thrust as he took off. The brook was far below them and she scarcely felt him land.

7 · NO PLACE TO GO

"No jumping for a long time," Mr. Jameson had said
and now Sally fully realized why. Young as she was she
was a very experienced rider and had often been asked
to ride for other people in shows, so she knew that no
horse could take solid fences at Phantom's speed and
not get into trouble—real trouble. Even if he stayed
up no judge in any show would give anything for such

a wild, uncontrolled performance. How often she had heard their admonition, "A good hunting pace, and the horse under full control at all times."

She had never had any trouble with Bay Boy on that score. Her problem had been to make him look like a free-going horse and to try to conceal the fact that he was timid at his fences. That had been difficult enough but this was something else and she was not sure if there was an answer.

She had realized from the first that to keep all that speed and power under control would be a long and difficult task. Now the jump at the brook had shaken her confidence after she had time to think it over. True, the horse was frightened, but that did not explain things entirely. There was something about the way he felt under her when he took off on that tremendous leap that made her realize this was his natural way of jumping. A line from an old English hunting song kept recurring to her: "You must have it at speed or not at all—" That may be the way it would always be with Phantom: "At speed—or not at all."

That night her dreams were all of Phantom and he was more than perfect, as a dream horse should be. He went like a leaf before the wind and floated over unbelievable fences effortlessly. So real was the dream that even on waking it still had reality and her worries of yesterday vanished.

Cantering through the woods Sally was happy and her mind was at ease. Now he was going as he should; fast, of course, but smoothly and easily. She felt he would respond readily if she asked for a slower pace and again in her mind she was on the outside course at a big show—Phantom going beautifully to an ever swelling applause.

Then she felt him gather himself—suddenly he was a coiled spring under her. A small dead tree had fallen across the path and he saw it! Sally's hair whipped behind her as Phantom took to the air as if Bechers itself were before him. He cleared the small tree in a huge sweeping arc and galloped on, eagerly looking for another jump.

Now she knew! The mere sight of a jump set him off—it lit a fire in him and he had to let go. If the fence was small he made it big; if it was big he made it bigger. That was the way he was; that was the way he always

Sally's hair whipped behind her as Phantom took to the air as if Bechers itself were before him. He cleared the small tree in a sweeping arc and galloped on, eagerly looking for another jump.

would be. The rules were not for him; he made his own rules.

Sally rode along somberly. The dreams were gone now. She would never be able to even keep him on an outside course at a show. At the pace he went it would be too small for him. Now no one would ever know how wonderful he was; how he could gallop and jump. He didn't fit anywhere.

Halfway home she met Mr. Jameson trotting along on a handsome chestnut horse. He pulled up and after greeting her said, "You look pretty serious. Is something bothering you?"

"I jumped him," she said. "I didn't mean to," and she told the whole story.

Mr. Jameson nodded. "He went very fast and jumped big?"

"Yes," she said, "he certainly did. But I expected that. It didn't bother me; it was the way he felt under me when he saw the jump. He was all on fire! Never in a million years will he jump as they do in the show ring. It just isn't his way."

"Maybe I should have known," said Mr. Jameson, "but they don't often come like that. Like Man o' War who all but burst into flame at the mere sight of a race track. Many horses like to jump but very few like the big fences. Hardly any want the big ones bigger."

He turned to her seriously. "In a horse trade you often get less than you expected; often much less. You got more than you bargained for; a great deal more. For some people that could be as bad. Are you disappointed?"

"Oh, no. I love him. It isn't his fault he's like that. I only hoped that someday he could show people how wonderful he really is. Not for me—just for him."

"Good girl," said Mr. Jameson gently. "No trophy room with cups and ribbons to show off. That's not for you." He was silent and thoughtful for a moment and then said, "He doesn't fit in anywhere now but don't give up. You can't give up on a horse that has too much. You may have to raise your sights a little—aim a little higher."

8 • THE MAN WHO KNEW HORSES

As Sally rode along she was studying Phantom; intently watching his every move. The way his ears flicked at anything that stirred, how his head came up when he was about to increase his pace. She must understand this horse so thoroughly that she would always know what he would do and why he did it. Nothing must ever surprise her; she must anticipate everything.

She was thinking of something Mr. Jameson had said as they rode along together the day before. He had dismounted and loosened the girth on his saddle and then removed a twig from under the pommel pad.

"How did you know it was there?" she had asked.

"He told me," answered Mr. Jameson. At her surprised look he explained, "I saw his skin twitch at the wither and then he looked back at me in a way that told me something was wrong."

"He really did tell you, didn't he?" said Sally. "I'm afraid I wouldn't have noticed."

"There was a time when I wouldn't have either but a fine horseman taught me to really study my horse. 'A horse can talk to you if you understand,' he used to say. And they talked to him. They knew he understood. That man could take a horse that others couldn't handle and ride him on a snaffle with a loose rein. You couldn't see what he did; he didn't seem to do anything, yet for him the toughest were like a ladies' pet hack. It must have been that in some way he let them know that he was a friend and understood them. They trusted him at once."

"He must have been wonderful," said Sally.

"He was. The best. The finest horseman I have ever known. I was lucky to have him for a teacher. He could tell things about a horse by watching him a few minutes that an owner might know only after having the horse in his stable for months.''

Mr. Jameson was silent, thinking back. "I never knew if it's what he saw or what he felt; a sort of instinct, but he knew a horse was going lame when others saw nothing wrong. Not even the vets. Anyone would know something was wrong if a horse nodded as he went along or pointed a leg in his stall but Mr. Marshall saw it long before that. I asked him how he knew but he couldn't quite put his finger on it. I think myself that he was so close to them that when they felt pain he felt it too.''

"He must have been wonderful! How I would have loved to know him.''

"They come like that only once in a while. Tom Whitcomb has an Irishman in charge of his stable that has something of what Mr. Marshall had. A sort of insight that lets him know how a horse feels and what he thinks. Joe Tanner is his name. You'll meet him sometime around at the shows.''

Sally turned to Mr. Jameson and spoke very earnestly. "That's the way I've got to be with Phantom. I feel it's my only chance with him. To understand him so well that I always know what he will do and why. So well that he will know it too."

"You sometimes surprise me," said Mr. Jameson with a smile. "So young and so sensible."

Sally laughed. "Maybe I seem silly to take it all so seriously but I can't help it. I've always been gone on horses ever since I can remember. I can never think of them as animals. They always seemed like people to me and they still do. More than ever since I've had Phantom. He's not only a person to me but a very special person. Proud and brave and with such spirit—" Words failed her.

"You know what I'd call him if he didn't already have a name? 'Shining Armor'! That's the feeling he gives me."

Mr. Jameson looked at her seriously. "You really love the horse, don't you?" he said gently. "When you feel like that it comes through. And don't think Phantom doesn't know it. There may come a time when you'll have to ask him—really ask him. Don't worry when you do. He'll give you all he has—and maybe a little bit more."

9 • ON HIS WAY

SALLY pulled Phantom up after coming out of the woods. She was pleased and happy. He had gone well —fast of course, he seemed to have no other pace, but sensibly, for him. He had slowed down for the sharpest turns of his own accord and seeing this Sally's spirits rose. When she saw he was willing to stop and rest for a moment she patted his neck and said, "You can't go on forever, Phantom. Not even you. Now rest a minute."

Soon she heard the steady beat of a slow canter, muffled by soft turf, and in a moment Mr. Jameson rode up.

"This I never expected to see," he said. "The Iron Horse willing to take a breather."

"It took time, though," said Sally. "Five miles, or maybe six."

"You'd never know it to look at him," said Mr. Jameson. "Not a wet hair on him."

"He does it so easily," said Sally. "Bay Boy would be in a lather with only half that much galloping."

"It's his stride," said Mr. Jameson. "I've been watching him. I never saw a horse reach out so, even when he's going easily. He just skims over the ground without effort."

"I was wondering if it was only my imagination," said Sally, "but I've never ridden a horse that gallops as he does. Not even Golden Boy, and he was champion at the Garden. I rode him once when his regular rider was sick, but even he didn't give me the feeling Phantom does. That he can do anything; anything in the world that he wants to."

Mr. Jameson looked at Sally intently. "So you feel that too?" he said, almost to himself. "He's got you too."

Sally looked up in surprise. "You think that?" she asked. "I thought it was only me."

Mr. Jameson nodded. "You've got something here that comes along only once in a while—once in a long, long while. A horse that always wants to give more than you ask for. Only the great ones have that."

A thrill ran through Sally as she listened.

"A horse that has that belongs on the track," continued Mr. Jameson, "and he will have none of it. He can jump like a deer but he can't be rated. No horse living can jump at his speed—it would be pure suicide. So where do we go?"

A bleak despair settled over Sally.

Mr. Jameson saw her dejection and hurried on. "But it isn't really hopeless. It's only that a lot must be done before you have a chance of showing what he is. I know you want that. For him to leave his mark."

"Oh, I do!" said Sally eagerly. "I feel he's sort of wonderful and I want everyone to see it. Not for me," she said earnestly. "Not because I own him. Just because of what he is."

"I never saw a horse reach out so, even when he's going easily. He just skims over the ground without effort."

"Then it's not impossible," said Mr. Jameson. "I remember Mr. Marshall once said, 'With enough patience you can put anything into a horse—anything but speed, courage and stamina.' That doesn't leave Phantom out, does it?"

"It certainly doesn't," said Sally. Her spirits rose. "I'll do anything I can—anything at all," she said earnestly.

"I know you will. You're already doing it. You're so close to him you don't realize what you've already accomplished. He's already a far different horse than the one that came off that van two months ago."

"You really think so?" asked Sally and a surge of happiness came over her. "You see that much difference?"

"A month ago I'd have said he would never be anything but a hack for a very bold rider. And by himself, with never another horse near him. But now—" he stopped and looked Phantom over carefully.

Sally waited breathlessly.

"Just go on as you are," said Mr. Jameson, "and we'll see."

10 • "YOU MUST HAVE IT AT SPEED
OR NOT AT ALL"

SLEEPING or awake the problem of Phantom was always on Sally's mind; how to use all that power and speed and spirit. There must be a way. The more she was with the horse the more she became aware of his qualities—not only his power and speed but something else that was hard to define. It was more than spirit and pride. Underneath was an honesty that was

very intense—integrity, that was it. In spite of his fiery
independence she knew she could always count on him
never to do anything mean or tricky. Never did she
have to watch out for his teeth or heels nor worry that
he would try to throw her. Everything was out in the
open. It was as if he had a code of his own that gov-
erned him. Obedience was not included but all the
other virtues were there. As Sally came to realize this
she loved him with a deeper affection than she had ever
felt for a gentler horse.

By now they understood each other and riding over
the countryside was pure joy. It was still always on his
terms—speed—as much speed as the going would take.
Although he yielded a little to reins and voice she knew
it would only be a little.

Never for a moment did she forget Mr. Jameson's
advice to study Phantom so that she would know him
as well as she knew herself. He had said this was her
one chance; her only chance, and she knew that he was
right.

They came to a very sharp turn in the bridle path
and Phantom shortened stride. He barely made the
turn and his stride was awkward and choppy. Her
heart skipped a beat! He had gone lame! Gone was that
effortless flowing stride; she was jolted about in the

saddle. Panic-stricken she tried to pull up but now the path ran straight for a long stretch and with a shake of his head he was off with that reaching stride that made the trees flow by in a swirl of green. No trace of lameness now! Sally understood. That was the way he was made! He had to be fully extended to go his natural pace, and only at that pace could he use the great power that made his stride so long and smooth. It wasn't possible for him to change that rhythm. The deep, sloping shoulder she admired so much called for speed; anything else was strange and unnatural for him.

Now she knew! Before she had not really believed that he was like a car with only one speed—it was just a fanciful thought that came to her. She had been sure it was only his temperament and that with patience it could be changed. Now she knew it never could.

"You must have it at speed or not at all." That was really the way it was. And what could she do with all that speed? Not the track; he wouldn't have that. Not the show ring—she could hear the splinter of rails as he hit a fence like a runaway car. There was nowhere to go! No one would ever know how grand he was; what power and drive there was, and eagerness to give everything he had.

She quickly rubbed her sleeve over her eyes. If that was the way it had to be then it would be only for her. It would be enough for her to know what he was— what he might have been. She had only to close her eyes and she could see the printed page: "and of all Native Dancer's fine sons one of the finest was Phantom."

But now they were out of the woods and he was in full gallop. The wind which whipped her hair till it streamed behind her sang, "Speed—speed or not at all."

11 • THE SMASHER

As they came over a rise she saw a man in the next field at work. He had just put up a post and rail jump and as they approached she saw he was piling brush in front of it. Phantom snorted and danced sideways at the sight of the jump.

"That's a keen horse," said the man. "He looks as if he had a real 'lep' in him." There was the lilt of an Irish brogue to his words.

"He has," said Sally, "but he's too fast at his fences. I can't rate him."

"If he stands back at them that won't hurt him," said the man with his eyes still on Phantom. "Not if he can jump to his looks. Mr. Whitcomb has one like him. A grand jumper but he must have his fences at speed. These fences are to school him over. With all that brush in front he can't get in too close, and that's the real danger with that sort. A week or two at these fences and he'll stand back and jump big."

Phantom snorted again as he looked at the fence and danced in a widening circle.

"He loves his fences, that one," said the man. "Better let him have it. It will ease him."

"It can't do any harm," thought Sally as she swung him in a wide circle and turned him toward the fence. Phantom's head came up and Sally felt the quiver of excitement that ran through him. When she felt the powerful thrust of his quarters as he took off she was sure he was too far away but he soared over the fence like a bird in flight and landed far beyond it. As he

When she felt the powerful thrust of his quarters as he took off she was sure he was too far away but he soared over the fence like a bird in flight.

galloped Sally felt the surging excitement that possessed him. As she swung him back toward the man
she could see the wide grin that lighted up his face.

"Glory be!" he cried out. "It's The Smasher himself
re-born. I never expected to see his likes again in this
life."

"The Smasher?" said Sally. "Who was he?"

"The greatest jumper that ever looked through a
bridle," said the man. "Big and black, he was, and
more than a horse. The world was too small for him
and he tried to make it bigger."

Sally felt a thrill run to her finger tips. That was
Phantom! That was him exactly! She listened breathlessly.

"They tried to make him gallop and jump like other
horses," said the man, and a rapt look came into his
face, "but that was not for him. He would have none
of it. It had to be his way or nothing. Then a bold lad,
wild as a leprechaun got hold of him and away they
went. Nothing could stop them.

"They were just alike, those two," he continued.
"No speed was too great and no fences too big. The
year he won the National I was standing below Bechers
and saw them come over that brute of a fence, clean.
Not brushing through, mind you, and that young

scoundrel sitting on him grinning like he was riding through the gates of heaven. Men have been killed at that fence but those two took it like it was a haycock in a field."

Sally's eyes glowed. "And you think my horse is like that," she said breathlessly. "Something like that."

"He is," said the man. "It gave me quite a turn to see him come over that fence. Making it bigger than it was just for the joy of it."

He turned to her very seriously. "That gray horse," he said, "has his own way of doing things. It may not be a safe way but it's the only way for him." Then he added, "But it's no horse for a young girl."

"I love him," said Sally simply. "I love the way he is. I'm not afraid. I trust him."

The man looked at her earnestly and Sally saw how kindly his weatherbeaten face was.

"If that's the way it is, then good luck, and ride him as if you knew he could never make a mistake. He'll know. That could save you both."

12 • AS IF HE COULD NEVER
MAKE A MISTAKE

"THAT would be Joe Tanner," said Mr. Jameson when Sally told him about it as they met each other riding through the woods the next day. "He had charge of Bob Whitcomb's horses. As fine a horseman as ever came out of Ireland. And he liked your horse?"

"He said he was like a famous jumper called The Smasher."

"The Smasher!" exclaimed Mr. Jameson. "What a

horse! No one could handle him but a young fellow named O'Brien. For him that black horse won everything in sight. Broke the record in the National, just galloping. And Joe Tanner thought Phantom was like him?"

"Yes," said Sally.

"In every way?"

"Yes," said Sally. "He saw him jump."

"And what did he think was the answer?" asked Mr. Jameson.

"To let him do things his own way," said Sally. "To try to see things his way and go along."

"It's a way," said Mr. Jameson thoughtfully. "Maybe the only way. But it could be dangerous. You know that."

Sally nodded.

"Not the galloping. The jumping at that speed. And you will be jumping, I know."

"I've got to. I love riding, but jumping—" she gestured wide with her hands.

"I know," said Mr. Jameson. "I remember only too well how it was. Once it takes you there's nothing else. But if it's to be jumping he's got to stand back or else it would be pure suicide. I'll talk to Whitcomb and get permission for you to school over his fences."

"Oh, thank you," said Sally gratefully. "He jumped so wonderfully over them—so big, you couldn't believe it."

"But remember this," continued Mr. Jameson, "don't let him see another fence. Only those with the brush in front of them. There he can't get in too close. If he ever hit as he rose to a fence—" Mr. Jameson paled at the thought.

"I'll remember," said Sally. She hesitated. "Mr. Tanner said something I've been thinking about ever since. He said I'd be safest if I rode him as if I knew he could never make a mistake."

Mr. Jameson looked at her intently. "And you were to let him go his own pace?"

"Yes. Just go along with him. He said it was the only way."

"I've thought that might be the answer," said Mr. Jameson soberly. "I've been afraid that might be the answer. If Joe Tanner says it is then that's it."

He put a hand on her shoulder and she saw how kind his face was and she felt his concern. "But please be careful," he said, "at least as careful as you can be." He paused. "Still it may not be as bad as all that. With all his fire and love of speed he has a lot of sense—in his own way. It's not what a timid rider would call sense but still it's there. So maybe when he feels he's on his own he'll be more careful than if you were fighting him. Even the wildest horse on the prairie will never try to destroy himself."

Sally nodded. "Somehow I always feel he knows what he's doing. Even when he's excited and really flying. Maybe that's why he never frightens me or even makes me nervous. I really trust him."

Mr. Jameson smiled. "All the books on riding tell you about hands and legs, heels and reins, but the most important thing they can't teach you. It's what separates the top horsemen from the rest. He knows his horse and trusts him. When you trust your horse so completely that you are without fear he knows it. I don't know how, but he does. And when the chips are down that will count for more than you know."

13 · AT HIS OWN PACE

MR. JAMESON and Joe Tanner stood beside the first of the three post and rail panels set some fifty yards apart in the big field. They were four feet high, with brush piled in front of them. This gave them considerable breadth as well as height; an obstacle to make a horse take notice. Sally was galloping Phantom in a wide circle at the other end of the field.

"A grand horse," said Joe Tanner, "maybe a great one. But I wish it was a tough lad on him—one that wouldn't mind a cracked bone or two. The way that gray goes it could happen."

"I know," said Mr. Jameson. "I feel responsible. I got her into this and now I can't get her out. She loves the horse and is proud of him. She wants him to be something special. Not for herself—just for him."

"I thought that was the way it was," answered Joe Tanner. "She has that look," He paused. "She fits the horse, you know. They might go far."

"What were you thinking of, Joe?"

"The Foxhunter Challenge Cup," said Joe Tanner. "He needs big fences and a real pace. Three miles and twenty fences that really have to be jumped. It suits the gray."

Mr. Jameson looked pale and his voice was unsteady. "But those fences, Joe. Solid as iron. And a young girl like that."

"I know," said Joe Tanner. "It would be murder for some but not for her. She doesn't scare. Fear and her walk on different sides of the street."

"And you think that can save her?"

"It has before," said Joe Tanner. "Many and many a time."

Sally swung Phantom toward the fences. "Now, Boy," she said. "It's all yours."

Phantom's head came up as he saw the fences before him. He snorted loudly and was off.

"Steady," called Sally gaily, "steady, Boy."

The stride lengthened until the wind whipped Sally's hair streaming behind her.

"Steady," she called again in a calm voice.

Now they were near the first jump and, despite the pace, Sally felt that Phantom was measuring the distance and the fence. Three strides away she knew he was coming into it just right—too far away for most horses, but not for him. The power and lift of his thrust was pure joy for her. This was Phantom at his best!

He was over as if it were only a log in his path and driving for the next fence. The last one he cleared with almost a foot to spare and galloped back to the start, snorting and shaking his head with pleasure.

"How was he?" called Mr. Jameson.

The power and lift of his thrust was pure joy for her.
He was over as if it were only a log in his path.

"Wonderful!" she said, her face aglow. "Just wonderful! He felt as if he knew just what he was doing all the way."

"He did," said Joe Tanner.

"And you let him do it all on his own?" asked Mr. Jameson.

Sally nodded. "I just talked to him a little," she said. "Just to let him know I was there."

"He knew," said Joe Tanner.

14 • TWENTY FENCES — SOLID AS IRON

As the days went by Phantom grew hard and fit with a sheen of condition to his dappled coat. Sally felt something was in the air. Mr. Jameson and Joe Tanner were always on hand when she took Phantom over the fences each day and she could not fail to notice how intently they watched him. Still she did not give it too much thought—the pleasure and thrill she got from

Phantom's performance was enough for her. Each jump was a new experience and she never ceased to marvel at the tremendous arc of his flight. Never once did he put a foot wrong; not once did he so much as rap a top rail. He seemed to always come into his fences just right. If he was a little far away he never deigned to cut his stride and put in "a short one" as most horses would. He merely gathered himself for an extra thrust from those powerful quarters.

Then came a day when the big gray seemed more than a horse. The rhythm of his reaching stride and the soaring jumps seemed almost beyond belief to Sally. Surely no horse living could do more or do it better.

When she brought him back to where Mr. Jameson and Joe Tanner were standing she could see by their faces that they shared her enthusiasm.

"That really was something!" said Joe Tanner. "If I ever saw anything better I can't remember when. That gray horse—" he shook his head in disbelief. "He just ain't human."

"How many times have you jumped these fences?" asked Mr. Jameson.

"Every day since you told me I could," answered Sally. "About three weeks."

"About sixty fences," said Mr. Jameson. "Has he ever made any mistakes? Hit one or made a bad jump?"

"Never," said Sally. "He always takes them the same. Always fast and he always jumps big—bigger than he needs to. But today—" She stopped and her face was aglow.

"Very special," said Joe Tanner. "Did you do anything different?"

"No," said Sally, "not really." She seemed a little flustered. "Maybe I talked to him a little more."

"And what did you say?" asked Joe Tanner.

Sally flushed. "I just said, 'Make this good. Make this very good.' "

"He heard you," said Joe Tanner.

Mr. Jameson spoke at last. "You want to do something with this horse," he said. "Something to show what he is."

"Oh, I do," said Sally. "He's really so wonderful. He deserves it."

"It won't be easy," said Mr. Jameson very seriously. "No show ring or outside course, you know. He's not geared for that. It will be twenty fences—big fences—at racing speed. A mistake could be dangerous."

"He won't make mistakes," said Sally eagerly. "He just can't. He's got so much—you can't realize what

he's like until you're on him—and there's always more
if you want it."

She turned to Mr. Jameson earnestly. "Maybe he
looks as if he's rushing his fences terribly but he isn't
—not for him, he isn't. He's measuring them all just
like any good jumper. Only fast—so fast you don't
think so. But when you're on him you know."

Joe Tanner turned to Mr. Jameson. "She's right,
sir," he said. "I don't see how she'd know at the pace
he goes but she's dead right." He turned to her.
"You're never nervous or frightened when he comes
into a fence like that?"

"No," said Sally. "How could I be with a horse like
that? There's nothing he can't do."

Joe Tanner turned to Mr. Jameson. "Doesn't the
good book say something about faith moving moun-
tains? So much faith ought to move a silver cup from
there," and he pointed to the east, "to here."

15 • BUCCANEER

SALLY sat beside Mr. Jameson in the big car as they drove through the green rolling countryside. Her hands were tightly locked together and the knuckles showed white. Mr. Jameson looked over and saw the pale set face.

"It's really not that bad," he said gently. "It's only a race. You know your horse and you know he can do it." He turned slightly, taking his eyes off the road for a moment. "And don't forget this—he knows it too."

Sally's face showed a strained smile. She turned to Mr. Jameson. "That's what Joe Tanner said. Do you really think he knows? How much I trust him? Do you honestly feel he knows?"

Mr. Jameson nodded. "He knows. I'm sure of it. I've seen that look in his eye. You don't see it often— maybe because people don't give enough. It doesn't come free; you have to earn it. I remember a horse that had it—he had it all." His eyes seemed to look far beyond the winding road.

"Oh, tell me," said Sally. "Tell me about him."

He looked over quickly and saw that the tension had left her face.

"He was the first horse I ever owned," began Mr. Jameson. "I could never have had him except that he was too much for his owner. He was big—very like Phantom in conformation and disposition. He had to have his own way. It was no use fighting him; he was so big and powerful and quick as a cat. If he didn't want you to ride him you had better not try. I was young and tough, then, and a good rider, but he almost killed me. Then one day he got a bad case of colic that brought on a high fever. The vets couldn't seem to do anything. He lay in his stall and thrashed around so violently in his pain that it looked as if he might destroy himself."

"Oh, how terrible!" said Sally, her eyes wide with apprehension. "What did you do?"

"I found that if I sat in the straw and took his head in my lap I could quiet him a little. There wasn't much I could do but talk to him and hold him so tight he couldn't struggle too much. I'd rub his head and neck with a towel; the sweat poured off him in his pain. Finally, after hours, when it all looked hopeless, the pain eased and I could rub him down and cover him with a blanket. We must have both fallen asleep for the next thing I knew the sun was shining through the stable window and he began to stir. Then he got up and the colic and fever were gone."

"How wonderful!" exclaimed Sally. "You stayed with him all night?"

"Of course," said Mr. Jameson. "Wouldn't you?"

"Oh, I would," she said.

Mr. Jameson paused, then went on. "You know he was a different horse after that. For me, he was. I don't know how he would have been for anyone else; he was my horse and no one else ever rode him. He never again bucked with me and he was the most perfect ride I've ever known. It was almost as if he were trying to read my mind, he was so eager to do what I asked."

Sally's face glowed. "Oh, that was wonderful! He must have been a grand horse."

"He was. When you win the Cup today look on the back where the names of the previous winners are engraved. When you see the name Buccaneer you will know. That was him. He stood the hardest drive I ever saw for the last quarter of a mile and wouldn't quit. It nearly killed him but he got his head in front at the finish. It took everything he had—he was never the same afterward. And he did it for me. I know that. He remembered that night and he did it for me."

16 • RIDERS UP

SALLY stood with Phantom in the roped-off enclosure that served as a paddock. In the enclosure were six other horses and riders. Two of the riders wore racing silks: one red with a white Cross, the other yellow with black sleeves.

"They're from the big tracks," said Joe Tanner, standing beside her. "Not really stake horses but pretty good. The owners must want that cup real bad to bring them down here. Usually it's just for point to point horses and top hunters."

"They look awfully fast," said Sally tensely as she watched them wheeling about as the grooms held them.

"I heard they were going to be here," said Joe Tanner, "so I thought we'd better make sure we weren't fooling ourselves about our horse. I timed him a quarter the other day."

"How was it?" asked Sally anxiously. "Was it fast enough?"

"It was. If he can carry that speed for three miles he can win here—and almost anywhere else."

"Oh, I know he can," said Sally earnestly. "He can go on forever. He's just—" She stopped, at a loss for words.

"I think he can too," said Joe Tanner. "He does it so easily. So there it is. Your only worry is to stay out of trouble and if he's what I think he is you'll be out all by yourselves. Only watch him on the turns. With his speed he could go wide and off the course. Try for the middle panel—even if it's the highest. Especially on that first turn. Mr. Jameson was worried about that one. It swings right-handed mighty sharp and a big striding horse like him could go wide and miss the flag."

"I'll be careful," said Sally, trying hard to keep her voice steady.

"One thing more," said Joe Tanner. "Watch those two," gesturing toward the two in silks. "They've been around and know all the tricks. Don't be near them coming into a fence. They'd try to get your horse to jump too soon and bring you down."

"What would they do?" asked Sally apprehensively.

"Often these jumping jocks yell 'Up' to their horse when they want them to take off and it can carry another horse with them. If he's behind a length, or even half a length he won't make it."

Then seeing Sally's pale face he said quickly, "But don't you worry. This fellow has the speed to lead all the way."

"Riders Up" came the call and Joe Tanner stooped and cupped his hands for Sally's foot and swung her lightly into the saddle. Phantom quivered with eagerness, nostrils distended and eyes wide and glowing. He danced sideways under Sally's light restraint. She patted his neck with a trembling hand. Joe Tanner noticed.

"It will all go after the first fence; then you'll see things sharp and clear. Let him stretch his legs for a turn on the way to the start over there." Sally looked down at the kindly weather-beaten face and tried to smile.

"Thank you," she said. "Thank you for everything. You've taught me so much. I'll always remember it."

Phantom started off in his sweeping gallop and she swung him in a big half circle toward the starting flag.

When Sally lined up she was aware that the other riders were studying Phantom intently. Particularly she noticed the hard shrewd eyes of the rider in red silks and it made her uneasy. She did not like his look —a little shiver ran over her. But there was not much time to think about it for Phantom was more than a handful. He knew what was coming and it was almost impossible to keep him back.

At last the six were almost in line and she heard the starter shout "Go!"

17 • WIDE ON THE TURN

EVEN on the turf the hoofs of the six racing horses were like a distant roll of thunder. The first fence grew larger and then it loomed before them—four chestnut rails to each panel, big and solid. Phantom was over like a bird and striding on before she heard the sharp rattle of rails as a horse rapped the top one. Suddenly she was as cool and collected as if she were schooling Phantom over the brush fences at home. He was going very fast but after the first wild rush she felt he knew what he was doing. He knew the fences were there and not to be trifled with and he was measuring them.

The next fence was on rising ground and so it looked very big but Sally's blood was up and she felt nothing was too much for Phantom. He could do anything! Her heart rose with the horse as his powerful drive carried them over and beyond the fence in a sweeping arc. If she had any doubts they were gone now. Only a wild exultation remained. "Oh, Phantom!" she cried aloud.

Then ahead she saw the fence on the turn that Joe Tanner had warned her about. A crowd had gathered there for it was the biggest fence on the course and she could now see how sharp the turn was. She swung Phantom in toward the center of the fence but he was going at such a pace that she realized that the best she could do was take an outside panel.

Suddenly something came into Sally's vision that made her heart seem to stop! A bright red balloon was bouncing over the turf pursued by a small child. He was running directly into Phantom's path.

Frantically Sally pulled on the left rein with all

Frantically Sally pulled on the left rein with all her strength and Phantom swerved sharply and careened off the course.

her strength and Phantom swerved sharply and careened off the course. They were beyond the fence and she saw the flag that marked the boundary line of the course as they swept outside it.

Tears blinded Sally's eyes. Now they were done for! A moment before Sally knew nothing could beat them and now it was over. They swung in a wide arc for Sally was still pulling on the left rein with the same desperation. Then she felt Phantom driving as never before. Through streaming eyes she saw the fence on the turn loom up. Phantom had swung back on the course! Surely no horse living could jump such a fence at that speed! Then in a wild, unbelievable flight they were over and in pursuit of the field, far far ahead.

"It's no use, Phantom," she cried but the big horse was like one possessed and drove on. Another fence at the same impossible speed and now the field was closer —much closer.

"You're wonderful, Phantom!" cried Sally, and the words were blown away. "Just wonderful, but you can't do it. Don't kill yourself!" The gray horse only

"Up!" screamed the rider in red and as his horse rose to the fence she felt Phantom take off. "Too far away" flashed into her mind, but it was too late.

drove on with another burst of speed. Now the field was coming back to them fast—fast, as Sally saw with unbelieving eyes. They were almost up with the stragglers. Suddenly she knew they had a chance. Even after what had happened they still had a chance.

"Come on, Boy!" she cried wildly. "You can do it! I know what you are, Phantom, but I want them to see it."

Now she could see the bay and the red silks clearly. The rider looked quickly over his shoulder and went to the whip.

Phantom needed no urging—he was running like a wild horse, and always the bay came closer. They were two lengths away—now one, and she saw the last fence before them.

"Up!" screamed the rider in red and as the bay rose to the fence she felt Phantom take off. "Too far away" flashed into her mind but the fence was below her and Phantom landed beside the bay. Now Phantom would not be denied and the bay knew it and fell back beaten. Sally's heart was all but bursting as they flew over the finish line all alone.

18 • PHANTOM KNEW

THE big silver cup was hugged so closely to Sally's heart that she was sure she could hear it ringing like a bell to that racing beat. Joe Tanner was rubbing Phantom's heaving sides. Then he threw a blanket over him and secured it. His practiced hands went over Phantom's legs gently.

"You were wonderful, Lad," he said softly. "When

you took that last fence I saw The Smasher again, full and clear. That's the way he did it—threw in all his blue chips at every fence." He ran the rub rag gently over the wet neck.

Mr. Jameson had gotten back for the presentation of the cup. He had been up at the turn and had seen the begining of Phantom's marvelous drive. Joe Tanner told him about the horse's jump at the last fence and it lost nothing in the telling.

"It just couldn't be done, sir. Never in this world, and there he was doing it. There wasn't time for her to be careful and there she was a full length back of the bay when that blasted fellow yelled his horse up. No horse could jump such a fence from that far back, but he did it—clean. I still don't see how he did it. He must have grown wings."

"Maybe he did," said Mr. Jameson. "In a way."

"I was standing right beside the fence," said Joe Tanner, and the wonder of it still shone in his face. "Do you know, sir, she knew he could do it? Any other rider would have known it wasn't possible but she never doubted he could do it."

"And the horse," said Mr. Jameson, "do you think he knew?"

"He knew," said Joe Tanner.